P9-DNN-226

To Alex, who always spots the
moon before I do —R.C.

For Mom —B.G.

Library of Congress Cataloging-in-Publication Data is available upon request.
ISBN 978-0-553-49707-6 (hc)
ISBN 978-0-553-49708-3 (lib. bdg.)
ISBN 978-0-553-49709-0 (ebook)

The text of this book is set in Brandon Grotesque.
The illustrations were rendered digitally.

MANUFACTURED IN CHINA
2 4 6 8 10 9 7 5 3 1
First Edition

CITY
MOON

written by Rachael Cole

illustrated by Blanca Gómez

schwartz & wade books   new york

In the fall,

when leaves are coming down,

it gets dark before we go to bed.

After dinner,

after tooth-brushing time,

we put on pajamas,

then coats and shoes.

We take keys,

and bang the big front door

behind us.

It's evening. It's night.
We are going on a walk
to look for the moon.

We crane our necks
up to the sky,
but it's hiding.
Where is it?

Oh . . . there it is!

The moon!

We stop and look,

but as we walk, it hides again.

We see glittery dots in the sky.
"Mama, are those other moons?"

"They're stars," says Mama.
Oh, *stars.*

We turn a corner.

"Mama, is that another moon?"

"It's the same moon.

There is only one moon," says Mama.

Oh, the same moon.

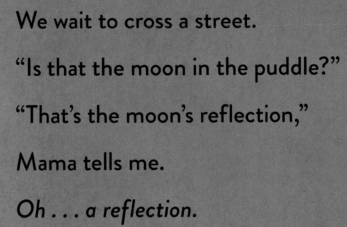

We wait to cross a street.

"Is that the moon in the puddle?"

"That's the moon's reflection,"

Mama tells me.

Oh . . . a reflection.

We take a step
and it's gone.
Where did it go?

GARAGE

Busy people walk in shadows.

Cars race home—

their lights flash and shine.

Fire engines speed and sirens wail.

We walk along with them,

heads up to the sky.

But where is the moon?

And then,

there it is.

Bright
and light
and round
and glowing.

We stop
and look.

"Mama, why doesn't everyone look?"

"They're busy," Mama tells me.

"Walking and riding bikes home
and cooking dinner
and putting children to bed."

"And it is also time
for us to go to bed,"
she whispers.

We walk home
and there it is—
rising high,
looking down,
before it hides
behind a cloud.

An airplane flies above.

Its red and white lights twinkle.

The cloud moves

and the moon peeks down at us.

We are yawning.

We climb the stairs and stand on the stoop.

We open up the door

and take off coats and shoes.

I climb into bed and see the moon.

"Can we keep the curtain open?"

Mama says yes, and whispers good night.